Woolly and Me

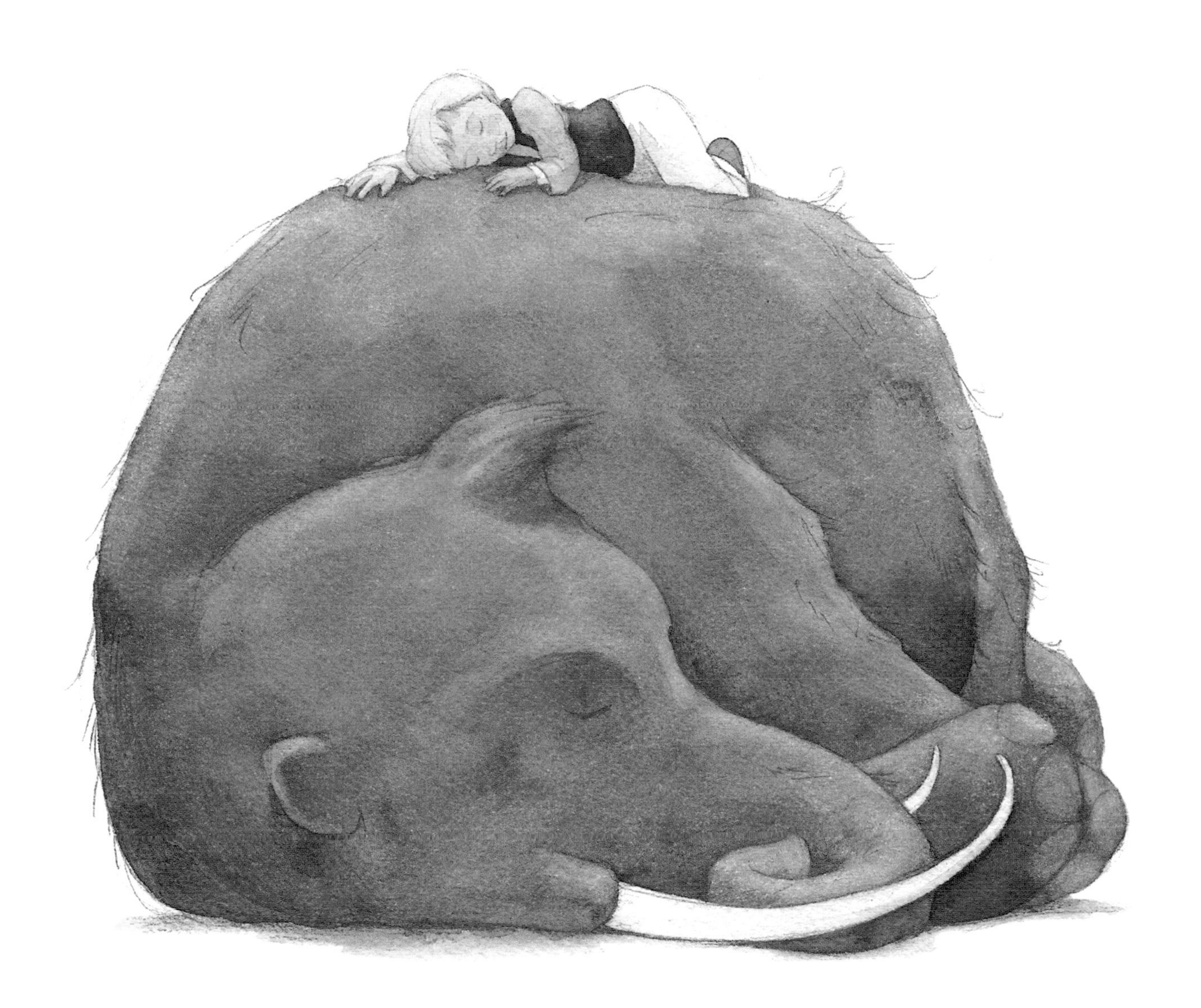

Quentin Gréban

TILBURY HOUSE PUBLISHERS, THOMASTON, MAINE

This is my pet mammoth Woolly.

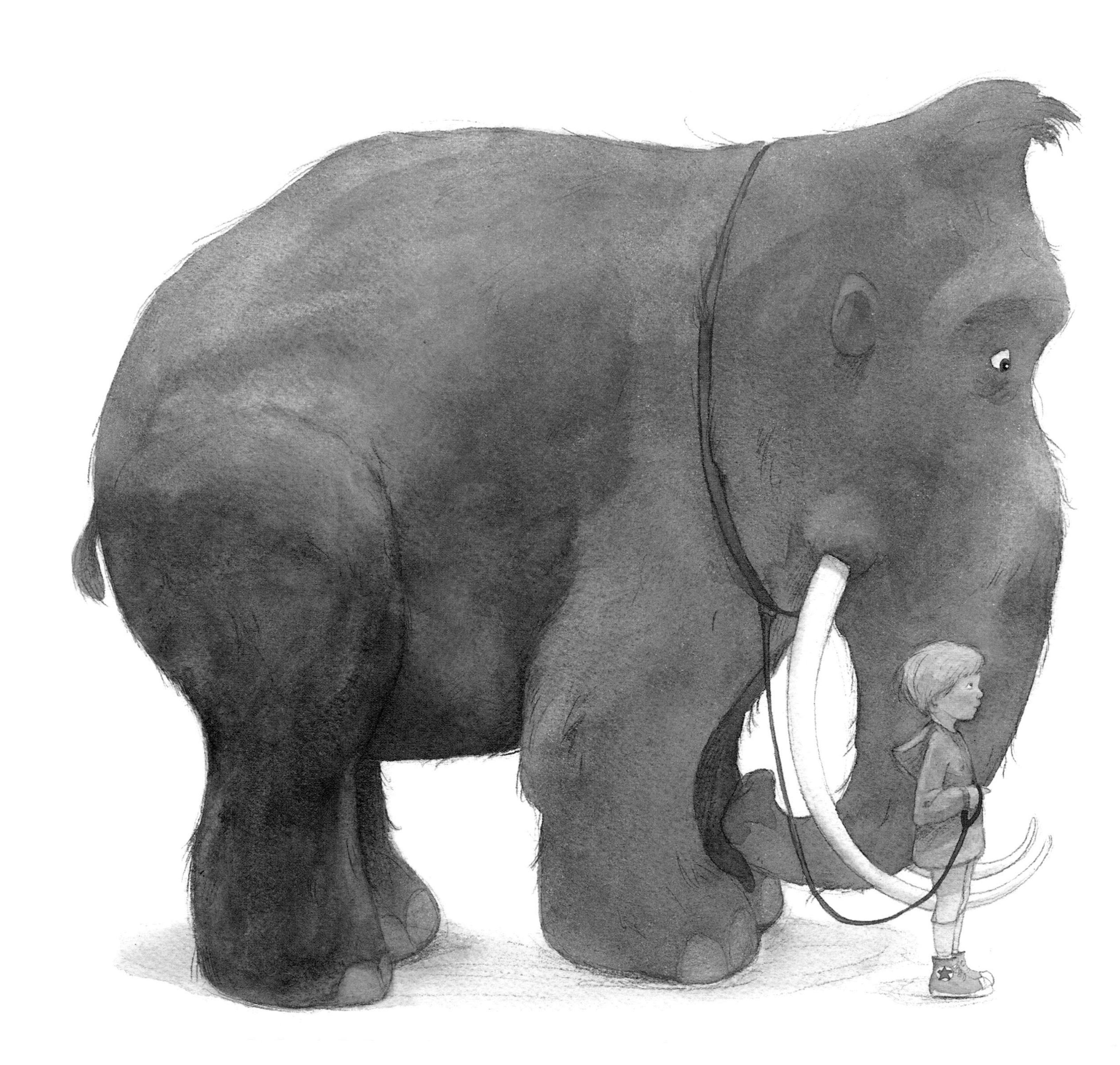

We go everywhere together.

He loves riding in the car.
It helps to have a convertible.

Soft
WAM
WAM

At the grocery store, I push Woolly in the cart . . .

. . . then he helps me carry the bags to the car.

Woolly has good table manners—well, almost.

After his bath, he sits while I brush his hair.

Woolly goes to bed when I do.

He's not afraid of monsters when I'm in the bottom bunk.

He likes to go to ballet class with me,
even though he looks a little silly in a tutu.

Woolly learned how to use
the bathroom in no time at all.

He's good at
playing hide and seek.

We have fun at the fair.

He gets scared on
the roller coaster,
but he feels
safer if I hug
him tight.

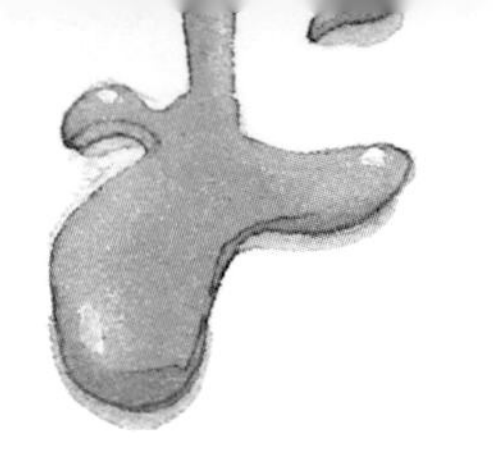

We paint together, too.

He's working on staying
inside the lines.

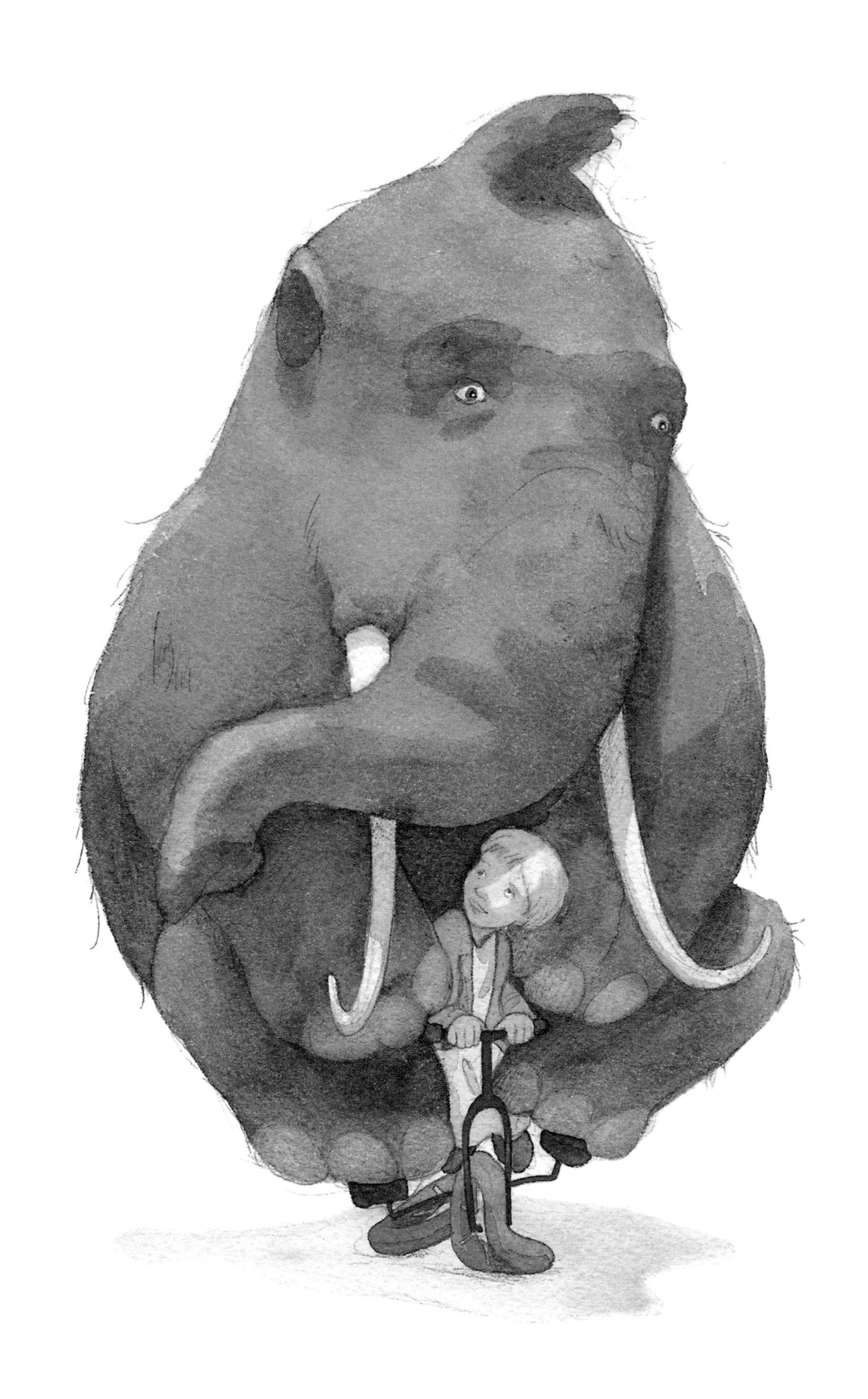

When we go bike riding, he pedals and I steer.

He feels better when I put
bandages on his boo-boos . . .

. . . especially when I
get a doctor's advice.

Some people might
not think he's real . . .

. . . but they don't know Woolly.

QUENTIN GRÉBAN was born in 1977 in Brussels, Belgium, and studied illustration at the Saint Luc Institute in Brussels. Since 1999, Quentin has published more than 40 children's books for French, Belgian, German, and Greek publishing houses. His books have been sold into Germany, Denmark, Hungary, England, Canada, Greece, Korea, the United States, and other countries. He received the Saint-Exupéry award in 2000 for *Les contes de l'Alphabet* (Editions du Jasmin), and his work was selected in 1999, 2001, and 2008 for the Annual of the Bologna Children's Bookfair. *Woolly and Me* has been published in 11 languages.

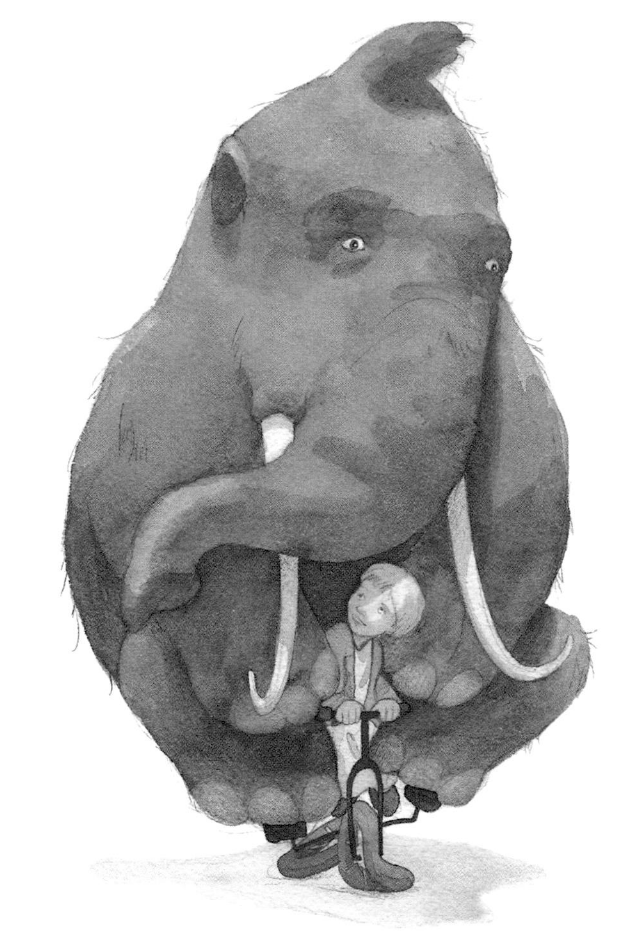

Tilbury House Publishers
12 Starr Street
Thomaston, Maine 04861
800-582-1899 • www.tilburyhouse.com

Hardcover ISBN 978-088448-636-7

First hardcover printing January 2018

15 16 17 18 19 20 XXX 10 9 8 7 6 5 4 3 2 1

Library of Congress Control Number: 2017953863

First published in 2012 by Mijade Publications as:

Cover and interior designed by Frame25 Productions
Printed in Korea through Four Colour Print Group, Louisville, KY